COMING HOME
BOOK 1

COMING HOME

P J Gray

SADDLEBACK
PUBLISHING

COMING HOME
BOOK 1

COMING HOME

SEARCHING FOR ANSWERS

THE TRUTH

SADDLEBACK
PUBLISHING
www.sdlback.com

ISBN-13: 978-1-62250-051-2
ISBN-10: 1-62250-051-2
eBook: 978-1-61247-709-1

Printed in Guangzhou, China
NOR/0000/CA00000000

17 16 15 14 13   1 2 3 4 5

Author Acknowledgments

I wish to thank Carol Senderowitz for her friendship and belief in my abilities. I wish to thank Linnea Johnson for her inspiration and dedication to learning. Additional thanks and gratitude to my family and friends for their love and support; likewise to the staff at Saddleback Educational Publishing for their generosity, graciousness, and enthusiasm. Most importantly, my heartfelt thanks to Scott Drawe for his love and support.

Her Son Returns

It was a sunny Saturday morning.

Nia was waiting for her son to come home.

He had been gone for several years.

Nia sat on her worn living room chair. She rubbed her hands as she waited.

Nia had cleaned her house from top to bottom.

She had washed the dishes. She had done the laundry.

Now she waited.

She looked at the TV but did not hear it.

Her mind was racing.

She looked at the clock on the wall.
It was almost ten o'clock.

Nia wanted to be happy, but she was afraid.

Would her son look different?

Would he act differently?

How had he changed?

His name was Will. He was her
only child.

Will left town after high school.

He owed money to many people.

Will would call Nia from the road sometimes.

He called last year from Florida.

He called last month from New York.

He said, "I want to come home."

Nia said, "Come home. Live with me. You can find a job here. I can help."

Homecoming

For the first two weeks, Nia was happy that Will was home.

He was home for dinner every night.

Will was smart and good with his hands. He fixed the stove.

He repaired the leaky faucet in the bathroom.

He made the lamp by her bed work again.

Will told her that he looked for work during the day.

She wanted to trust him. She wanted him to find a job.

Nia was afraid that he would call his old friends.

She did not want him to get in trouble again.

At night, he went out and came back
very late.

He began talking to a girl named Karyn on his
cell phone every day.

He liked Karyn.

Will got upset when Nia asked about Karyn.

"She is just a friend," Will said. "Don't worry about it, Mama."

"Is she nice?" Nia asked. "Does she have a job?"

"Yes, she paints fingernails," Will said.

"Will I ever meet her?" Nia asked.

14

"Stop asking so many questions!"
he shouted as he left the house.

The Girlfriend

Karyn worked in a nail shop near downtown.

She liked her job. She was good at it.

Karyn was young and pretty.

She was the best-dressed worker in the shop.

Her customers liked her.

Karyn hoped to buy her own shop one day.

Karyn's boss was named Eve.

Eve liked to wear her shirts and pants
too tight.

She also liked to wear bright colors.

Eve made sure that her nails were the longest
and brightest in the shop.

She hired Karyn three years ago.

Karyn's old boyfriend was Eve's brother,
Shawn.

Eve was sad that Karyn and Shawn were no
longer a couple.

Karyn and Eve got along, but Karyn did not
trust her.

The Other Man

Eve asked Shawn to come to the shop all of the time.

She asked Shawn to help her fix things that were not broken.

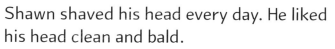

Shawn shaved his head every day. He liked his head clean and bald.

He liked to walk into the shop, remove his hat, and say, "Does anybody want to rub my head for good luck?"

Shawn would wink and smile when he said this.

The customers would laugh, but Karyn would look away.

Shawn looked and smiled at Karyn when he was in the shop.

Karyn got mad when he looked at her.

Karyn could not forget the things that Shawn did to her when they dated.

He hurt her.

Karyn wanted to be happy with Will.

She liked him.

Karyn wanted a better life.

She finished work and waited for Will by the front door of the shop.

When Will arrived, they kissed at the door.

Eve could see Karyn with Will, holding hands and kissing.

Eve got mad when she saw them.

Karyn and Will left the shop and walked next door to the food store.

Back at the shop, Eve called out to Shawn.

Shawn came out of the back room.

"What do you want now?" he yelled back.

"Do me a favor." Eve smiled. "Get me some lightbulbs from the store."

"Do you need them right now?" Shawn asked.

"Yes! I need them right now. Go!"

Mail Room Glory

Nia was ready to speak to her boss about a job for Will.

Her boss was Mike Baldwin.

He worked at a factory for many years.

His hair was gray by his ears.

Nia tapped softly on his office door.

"Come in, Nia. Sit down. What is on your mind?" he asked.

"Will has come home," she said.

"Really? Is he in trouble again?"

"No, I don't think so. He looks good."

"Do you need money?" Mr. Baldwin asked.

"No. I need a favor. He needs a job."

"I don't think we have anything to offer him."

"What about a job in the mail room?" Nia asked.

"I'm not sure if that is a good idea."

"Oh, please, Mike."

"I'm Mr. Baldwin, Nia."

"I am sorry, Mr. Baldwin. Please. Do this for me. I'll make sure that he is here every day."

"Okay, Nia," Mr. Baldwin said.

"You can trust him. I promise," Nia added.

"Okay, I will hire him. But you must promise me something," he replied.

"What, Mr. Baldwin?"

"You cannot tell anyone at work that he is your son."

"I promise," Nia said.

This Store Is Closed

Karyn and Will walked into the store.

They were happy and held hands.

"I need milk to bring home," Karyn told him.

"Okay, I'll stay here and look at some magazines," Will said.

She walked to the milk case at the back of the store.

Shawn walked into the store.
He passed Will.

Shawn looked around to find lightbulbs.

Then he saw Karyn and walked up to her.

"Hey, Karyn."

"What do you want?" Karyn asked.

"Nothing. I just wanted to see your pretty face," Shawn said with a smile.

"Here it is," she said as she pointed her finger to her face. "Now leave me alone."

Will looked up from his magazine and saw them.

He walked over to Karyn and held her hand.

"Is there a problem here?" Will asked.

"Who are you?" Shawn asked.

"He's my boyfriend!" Karyn said.

"Boyfriend? When did you get a boyfriend?" Shawn asked.

"It's none of your business," Karyn said.

"Do you have a problem with that?" Will asked Shawn.

"Do you want to take this outside?" Shawn asked Will.

"Stop it!" Karyn yelled. "Will, let's go."

Karyn left the milk in the case and walked with Will to the door.

At the door, Will turned to Shawn and yelled, "Talk to her again and I'll kill you."

Dinner Talk

Nia made Will his favorite dinner.

He loved chicken and rice.

She sat and ate with him.

He ate two bowls. He was full and happy.

After dinner, she said, "I am glad you liked it."

Will smiled at her and nodded his head.

"I found you a job," Nia said with a smile.

He asked, "What job?"

"It is in the mail room at the factory," Nia said. "You can start on Monday."

"I don't want to work there," Will said.

Nia asked, "Why not? Do you have another job?"

Will tossed his fork into his empty bowl.

He stood up, marched to his bedroom, and slammed the door.

Nia sat at the dinner table alone.

Nia did not know what to do.

Later, she cleaned the dishes and went to bed.

Her legs and feet felt so tired.

She rubbed some lotion on her hands and arms.

Her eyes were very heavy.

Will tapped on her bedroom door and opened it.

He said, "I will take the job."

Nia smiled at him from her bed.

He closed the door and went back to his bedroom.

Nia turned off the lamp next to her bed.

It was the lamp that Will fixed last month.

Watching and Waiting

Will had worked in the mail room for three weeks.

Sometimes he liked the work. But he would not admit that to his mother.

Most of the time, he was bored.

He tried to save some money, but he liked to spend it on Karyn.

Mr. Baldwin watched Will at work every day.

Will did not know that Mr. Baldwin watched him.

Mr. Baldwin had listened to Nia talk about Will for many years.

Will never knew that.

On his break, Will went outside to drink some coffee.

He saw a man drive slowly through the parking lot in a big dark car.

Will looked closer. The driver was Shawn.

When Shawn drove away, Will called Karyn on his cell phone.

"Hey, it's me," Will said.

"What's wrong?" Karyn asked. "You never call me at work."

"That guy you know," Will said, "he just drove past my work, staring at me."

"What guy?" Karyn asked.

"That guy from the store a couple of weeks ago."

Karyn could not speak. Her mind was racing. Shawn was dangerous.

"Hey, Karyn," Will said. "Did you hear me?"

"I have to go. I have a customer sitting here. I have to go," she repeated.

Karyn quickly hung up and stared at the empty chair in front of her.

She turned and looked over at Shawn's sister, Eve.

Eve was helping another customer and did not see Karyn looking at her.

Karyn was scared.

The Appointment

For three days, Nia called every nail shop in town.

She asked every shop if they had someone named Karyn working for them.

Nia finally found the right shop and made an appointment.

She lied to Mr. Baldwin so she could leave work early.

When Nia arrived, she spoke to Eve at the front desk.

"I have an appointment with Karyn at two o'clock," she said.

"Yes. Welcome, Nia."

Eve pointed at Karyn's table with her long bright-orange fingernail.

Nia walked over.

Karyn met Nia and began doing her nails.

They did not speak for a few minutes.

Nia kept smiling at Karyn.

Karyn asked, "Have we met before?"

"No," Nia said.

"Who gave you my name?" Karyn asked.

Nia had to think fast.

"Nobody. I just found the shop's name in the phone book," Nia said.

Karyn and Nia talked and got to know each other.

Karyn said, "You look like somebody I know."

"I hope that she is pretty," Nia joked. Then she laughed.

Karyn also laughed.

"No," Karyn replied. "It is not a woman. It is a man."

"A man?" Nia asked.

"Wait! I'm sorry. I didn't mean that you look like a man."

Nia laughed again and said, "It's okay, honey. I know what you mean."

They sat and smiled for a moment.

"Do you have a boyfriend?" Nia asked.

"Yes," Karyn said.

"And do you like him?" Nia asked.

"Oh yes. I like him very much," Karyn said. "He is good to me."

Nia smiled.

Karyn smiled back and asked, "Which color of polish would you like?"

"You can pick one," Nia said. "I'm sure that I will like it."

Karyn smiled.

The Truth

Mr. Baldwin had watched Will at work. He was not happy.

Will had not been doing a good job.

Mr. Baldwin asked Will to step into his office and shut the door.

"You have to be more careful,"
Mr. Baldwin said.

"I am careful," Will replied.

"And you were late to work many times,"
Mr. Baldwin said.

"That's a lie. You just don't like me," Will said.

"I do like you, Will."

Nia could hear them from her desk.
Their voices were getting loud.

She was upset and wanted to stop them.

Will opened the door and shouted,
"I quit!"

He marched past Nia and headed for the
back door.

Mr. Baldwin yelled, "Come back!"

Nia ran behind Mr. Baldwin as they followed
Will to the parking lot.

Mr. Baldwin stopped Will just outside
the back door.

"Will, listen to me," Mr. Baldwin said.

"Go to hell!" Will yelled.

Suddenly a big silver car drove past them in the parking lot.

The windows were not clear. They were black.

Mr. Baldwin, Will, and Nia watched the car window roll down.

A gun was fired from the car. *Pop*.

Nia screamed as she held on to the back door.

Two more shots were fired. *Pop*. *Pop*.

Will pushed Mr. Baldwin away to protect him.

Mr. Baldwin and Will fell to the ground.

The car drove away very fast.

The car tires smoked as it took off.

When Will moved, he saw blood on Mr. Baldwin's shirt.

Mr. Baldwin was shot in the chest.

Nia screamed, "Mike!"

She ran to him and dropped to her knees.
She held his head in her lap.

Will stood next to them. He could not speak.
He was in shock.

"Mike," Nia cried.

"Mike?" Will asked.

"Yes," Nia said to Will. "This is your father!"

About the Author

PJ Gray is a versatile, award-winning freelance writer experienced in short stories, essays, and feature writing. He is a former managing editor for *Pride* magazine, a ghost writer, blogger, researcher, food writer, and cookbook author. He currently resides in Chicago, Illinois. For more information about PJ Gray, go to www.pjgray.com.